BRAIN GAMES for Young Minds

3

MOONSTONE

Published in Moonstone
by Rupa Publications India Pvt. Ltd 2022
7/16, Ansari Road, Daryaganj
New Delhi 110002

Sales centres:
Allahabad Bengaluru Chennai
Hyderabad Jaipur Kathmandu
Kolkata Mumbai

ISBN: 978-93-5520-749-4

First impression 2022

10 9 8 7 6 5 4 3 2 1

1. Do the Chores

Do you perform these household chores too? Name them with the help of the box given.

Rake	Sow	Wash	Clean	Dust
Mop	Iron	Mow	Water	Sweep

_____ clothes

_____ clothes

_____ the plants

_____ seeds

_____ the wardrobe

_____ the floor

_____ the floor

_____ the leaves

_____ the lawn

_____ the furniture

2. Order It

Write the names of these things we wear and then number them in the alphabetical order according to the first letter.

____

____

____

____

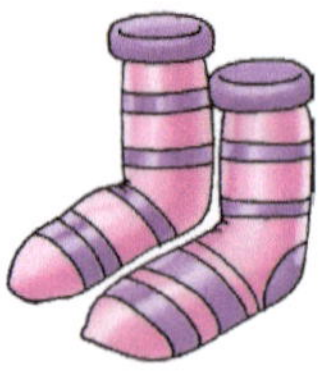

____

____

____

____

3. Circle It

Circle the correct answer and write in the space to complete the sentence.

1.

The elf is ________ the ball.

in / behind / on

2.

The elf is _______ the table.

beneath / in front of / under

3.

The elf is ______ the box.

in / out / into

4.

The elf is ______ the pillars.

beside / inside / between

5.

The elf is ________ the sofa.

in front of / behind / inside

6.

The elf is sitting _____ the lion's back.

on / in / over

4. Find Out

Find the following delicious desserts in the word search below and complete their names.

	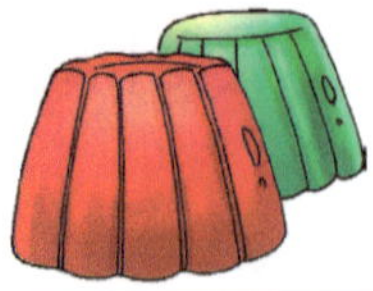	
J_m	Je_ _y	F_d_e
		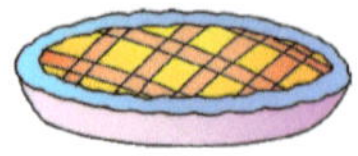
Tr_ff_e	P_st_ _	P_dd_n_

S_uff_e	B_ow_ _e	G_nge_ _r_ad

c	g	a	g	l	o	p	v	k	n	t	q	i	i	n
o	i	f	d	j	u	x	u	l	s	h	f	a	f	k
o	n	u	j	x	p	y	t	r	u	f	f	l	e	t
k	g	g	c	u	p	c	a	k	e	t	p	a	b	j
i	e	e	m	s	k	q	h	p	y	c	a	k	e	e
e	r	p	v	l	f	v	s	w	r	a	t	x	h	l
x	b	a	x	q	r	x	o	e	w	b	d	a	q	l
v	r	s	e	j	b	e	u	z	p	i	e	l	b	y
m	e	t	c	t	w	a	f	f	l	e	g	b	w	h
n	a	r	l	c	s	j	f	w	j	a	m	r	y	p
s	d	y	a	p	f	b	l	c	n	i	g	o	i	v
c	y	o	i	h	c	t	e	t	a	r	t	w	c	n
o	f	c	r	p	u	d	d	i	n	g	h	n	g	a
n	f	u	d	g	e	o	v	v	b	z	k	i	q	z
e	v	g	p	h	m	u	f	f	i	n	i	e	w	y

_ie	C_ _e	E_l_ir
	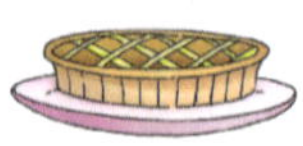	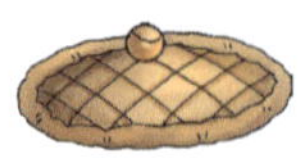
C_ _k_e	T_ _t	Wa_ _le

_ _ffin	_ _pca_e	S_ _ne

5. Fill Up

Write the plurals in the blanks.

Fox

____

Turkey

____

Potato

____

Volcano

____

Roof

____

Wife

____

Berry

____

City

____

6. Add Meaning to It

Put the words in the correct order to make meaningful sentences.

The is cat in hat the.

swimming The boy is.

The girl running is.

The cooking man is.

is The doll on chair the sitting.

bird The is flying.

7. Describe It

Circle the describing words.

Full moon

Big castle

Wicked witch

Good fairy

Sweet candy

Black cat

White ghost

Wild lion

Dark night

Long stockings

Haunted house

Scary spider

Round pumpkin

Hot soup

8. Complete It

Fill in the blanks using the picture clues.

3 

1 

5 

2 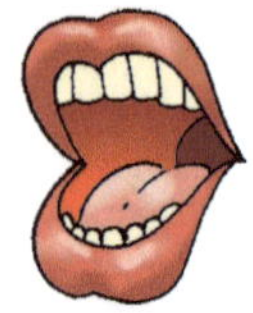

8 

4 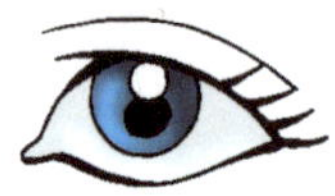

1. _ A I _
2. _ O U _ _
3. _ I _ _ E _ _
4. E _ E
5. _ O _ E
6. _ O _ _ U E
7. _ A _ _
8. _ O E
9. _ _ O _ A _ _
10. _ E _
11. _ E A _
12. A _ _

9 

6 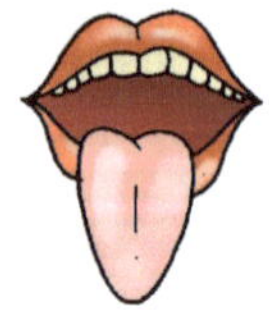

10 

7 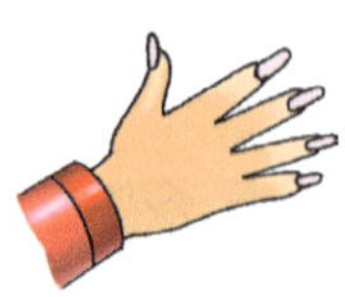

11 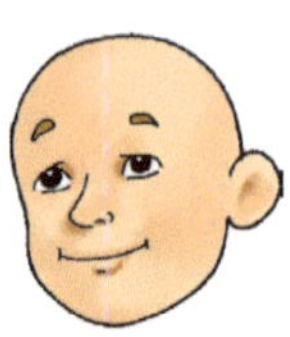

12 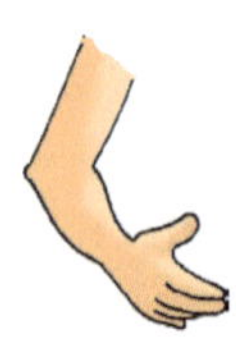

9. Fill Up

Use the words below to fill in the blanks.

loudly	bravely	slowly
quickly	carefully	happily

1. The tortoise walked ________.

2. The hare ran ________.

3. The rooster sang ________.

4. The king fought ________.

5. The prince and the princess danced ________.

6. The prince picked up the glass slipper ________.

10. Connect It

Draw a line and join the opposite words.

Tall

Loud

Slow

Dark

None

Short

Old

Quiet

All

Fast

Light

New

11. Circle It

Circle the correct answer.

A cow/An cow

A milkmaid/
An milkmaid

A hen/An hen

A egg/An egg

A elephant/An elephant

A leaf/An leaf

A camel/An camel

A desert/An desert

A ape/An ape

A rainforest/
An rainforest

A yak/An yak

A mountain/
An mountain

12. Find Out

Unscramble to find what these animals say.

RROA ____________

EOWM ____________

RBAK ____________

RCAOK ____________

UAQCK ____________

SSHI ____________

OOTH ____________

ELATB ____________

13. Write It

Fill in the missing vowels to complete the names.

H_E

S_ _DS

P_TS

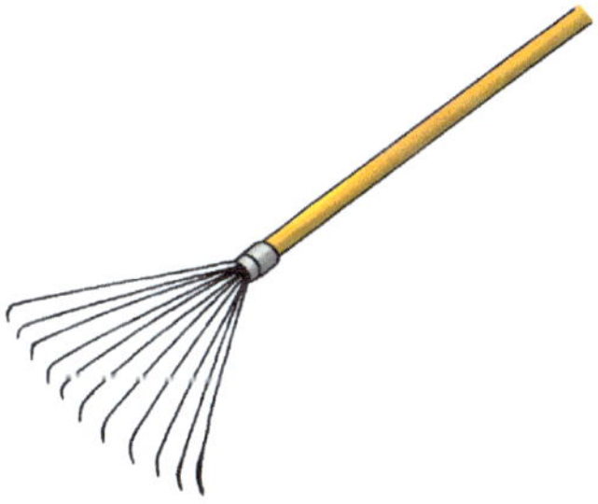

R_K_

W_T_R_NG C_N

SH_V_L

14. Name It

Little Red Riding Hood is in the forest and she is trying to remember the names of these flowers. Can you help her unscramble the names?

SORE

____

UNSFWELOR

____

ADHIAL

____

ISDAY

____

TIPUL

____

RLDMAIGO

____

ADFDILFO

____

15. Spell It

Circle the correct spelling.

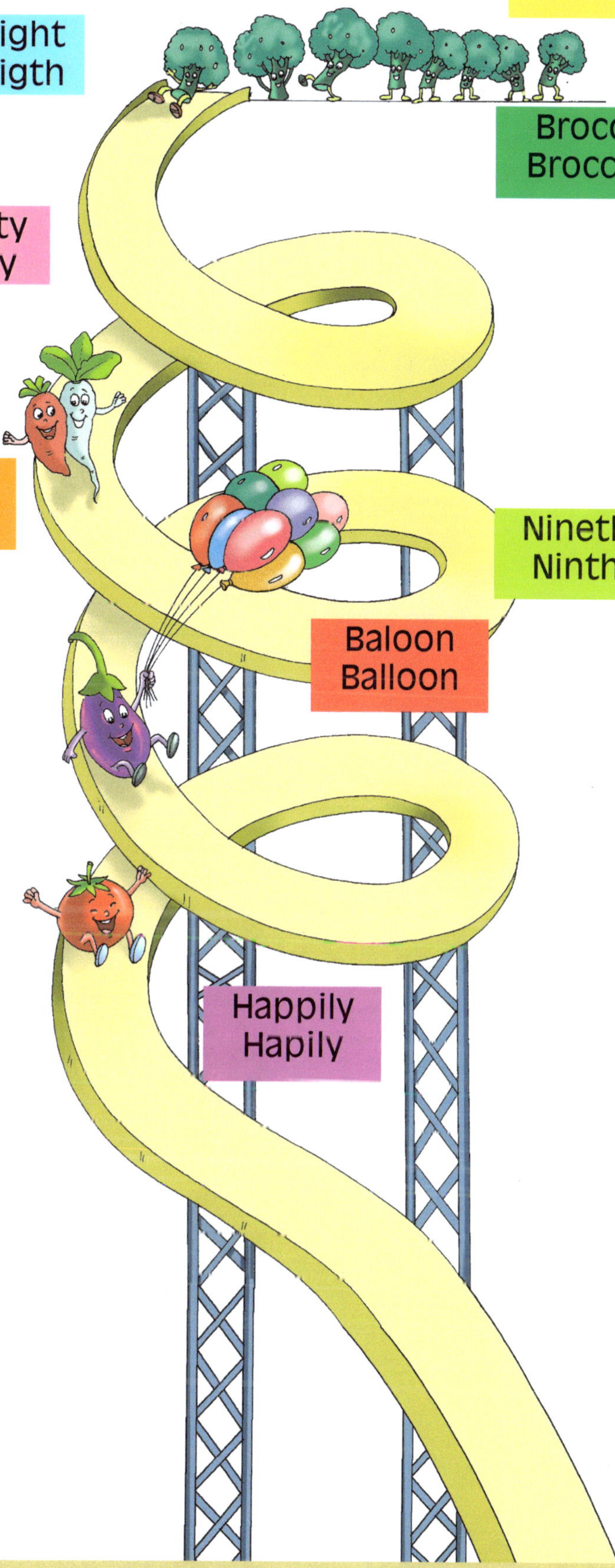

Eight
Eigth

Height
Heigth

Brocoli
Broccoli

Fourty
Forty

Friend
Freind

Nineth
Ninth

Baloon
Balloon

Happily
Hapily

16. Guess It

Look at the picture clues and guess the words.

1.  +  ____________

2.  +  ____________

3.  +  ____________

4.  +  ____________

5.  +  ____________

6.  +  ____________

7.  +  ____________

8.  +  ____________

17. Fill Up

Write C in the box for the objects that are countable and U for the objects that are uncountable.

18. Connect It

Draw a line and connect the words to the group it belongs to.

Telephone

Mount Everest

Gorilla

Computer

River

Tailor

Porcupine

Soldier

Name

Place

Animal

Thing

19. Circle It

Look at the pictures and circle the correct word.

Foal
Cub

Kitten
Calf

Piglet
Fawn

Gosling
Kid

Kit
Joey

Pup
Kitten

Nit
Tadpole

Fry
Larva

20. Crossword

Solve the crossword.

Across

1 

4 

7 

8 

9 

10 

Down

1 

2 

3 

5 

6 

21. Complete It

Fill in the missing letters to complete the words.

S_EE_

_US_

_AL_

_UM_

_LY

AUG

JU_G_E

CR_

_AN_E

LI_TE_

_EA_

_IC_

22. Group It

Name the objects and then group them.

Words beginning with A	Words beginning with B	Words beginning with C	Words beginning with D

23. Find Out

Find the words in the grid.

Wet	Open	Brown
Yellow	Silly	Round
Tall	Soft	Sleepy
Funny	Happy	Shiny
Hard	Tiny	Dirty
Playful	Dark	Young

			y	d	i	r	t	y			
		y	z	r	y	q	y	j	b		
	t	p	r	o	e	t	o	w	r	h	
v	f	l	g	u	l	s	u	p	o	a	y
x	t	a	f	n	l	o	n	c	w	r	a
t	a	y	u	d	o	f	g	f	n	d	v
i	l	f	n	g	w	t	h	a	p	p	y
n	l	u	n	p	d	a	r	k	h	w	z
y	b	l	y	l	o	p	e	n	g	e	o
	t	d	x	y	s	i	l	l	y	t	
		p	b	s	l	e	e	p	y		
			s	h	i	n	y	e			

24. Fill Up

What comes before, after and in the middle? Fill in the blanks with the correct letter.

_UV
C_E

RS_
_HI

J_L
N_P

I_K
MN_

L_N
OP_

S_U
FG_

KL_
_RS

_CD
H_J

25. Circle It

Look at the pictures and circle the correct word.

Flower | Flowers

Coat | Coats

Brush | Brushes

Butterfly | Butterflies

Zebra | Zebras

Fruit | Fruits

Bat | Bats

Bowl | Bowls

Block | Blocks

Horse | Horses

Queen | Queens

Fly | Flies

Snail | Snails

Ring | Rings

26. Crossword

Use the picture clues and solve the crossword.

Across

2 

3 

5 

Down

1 

2 

4 

7 

8 

9 

6 

9 

10 

27. Complete It

Fill in with the correct word.

He	She	It	We	They

1. The cat is sleeping.

   ______ is sleeping.

2. The boy is playing.

   ______ is playing.

3. Annie is reading.

   ______ is reading.

4. Susan is Tim's mother.

   ______ is Tim's mother.

5. Sam and I are playing.

   ______ are playing.

6. Sam and Rita are eating.

   ______ are eating.

28. Order It

Number the actions according to the order in which they happen.

1.

2.

3.

4.

29. Circle It

Circle the word that best completes the sentence.

1. The bride wore a beautiful ________.

ring

ring

2. A ________ hung on the tree.

bat

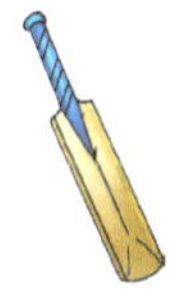
bat

3. Jim won the ________ prize.

second

second

4. I heard a dog's ________ .

bark

bark

5. I bought a new ________.

pen

pen

6. Humpty Dumpty had a great ________.

fall

fall

7. The girl has a ________ on her dress.

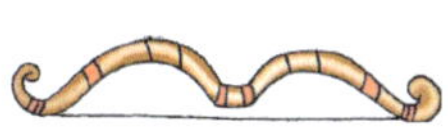
bow

bow

30. Find Out

Find the names of all the aquatic species given in the picture clues in the grid.

Coral

Whale

Seal

Stingray

Worm

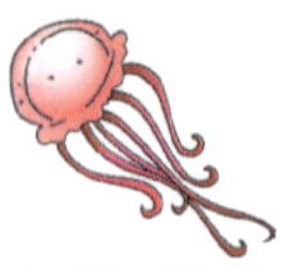
Jellyfish

Eel

Sea horse

Oyster

Clam

u	w	s	e	f	j	n	s
f	o	h	r	i	q	m	q
l	r	a	w	s	g	o	u
q	m	r	e	h	o	f	i
s	h	k	c	o	s	o	d
t	v	c	r	a	b	c	j
i	w	h	a	l	e	t	e
n	t	s	e	i	h	o	l
g	z	e	e	s	q	p	l
r	s	a	l	n	b	u	y
a	t	h	r	a	j	s	f
y	a	o	t	i	q	c	i
m	r	r	s	l	d	o	s
a	f	s	h	c	o	r	h
d	i	e	e	l	l	a	s
h	s	e	l	a	p	l	e
b	h	a	l	m	h	x	a
t	p	z	i	j	i	r	l
u	l	s	p	o	n	g	e
d	o	y	s	t	e	r	t

Snail

Crab

Starfish

Shark

Dolphin

Octopus

Fish

Sponge

Squid

31. Choose It

Look at the pictures and choose the correct answer.

crawl	run	swim	sting
climb	drive	jump	sing

1. Mimi can ______________.

2. The cat can ______________.

3. The rat can ______________.

4. Jim can ______________.

5. Father can ______________.

6. Amy can ______________.

7. Lizards can ______________.

8. Scorpions can ______________.

32. Name It

Look at the objects and complete their names.

H_US_

D_CT_R

T_G_R

P_INT_R

D_NK_Y

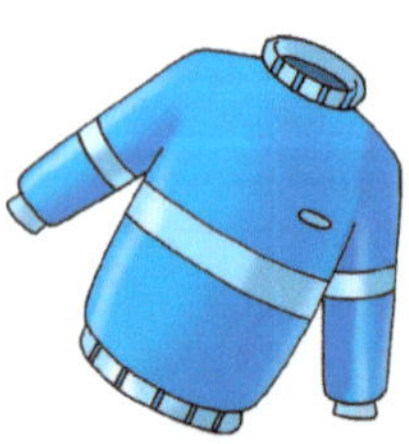

SW_AT_R

CL_CK

VI_L_N

L_BR_RY

CR_Y_N

J_IC_

BEDR_ _M

33. Connect It

Match the questions with the correct answers.

1.	Who lived in the sea?	A pea
2.	What did the emperor want?	New clothes
3.	What did the nightingale do?	A mermaid
4.	What did Snow White do?	It sang
5.	What was beneath the princess's mattress?	Cooked food

34. Circle It

Look at the pictures and circle the correct spelling.

one | won

bye | buy

pair | pear

flower | flour

hare | hair

bare | bear

which | witch

sew | so

stare | stair

be | bee

mane | main

night | knight

see | sea

weigh | way

35. Crossword

Solve the crossword with the help of the clues below.

Across

4. Has black and white stripes
6. Tallest land animal
8. Hopping Australian marsupial
10. Likes to chase mice
11. Like to roll around in the mud

Down

1. Fastest land animal
2. Starts life as a tadpole
3. Man's best friend
5. Large animals with a trunk
7. King of the jungle
9. Large animal with a horn

36. Fill Up

Use the clues below to decode the sentences.

1. 

2. 

3. 

doing = 

what = 

you = 

am = 

are = 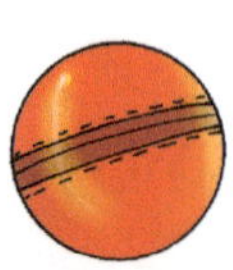

I = 

writing = 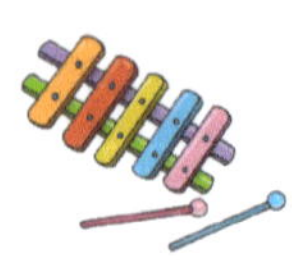

studying = 

dancing = 

37. Order It

Arrange the words in the correct order.

1. I a boy am.

____

2. am I girl a.

____

3. This cat is a.

____

4. cat is The chair under the.

____

5. fox The is in well the.

____

6. The barking dog is.

____

7. The flying birds are.

____

8. stars The shining are.

____

38. Rhyme It

Circle the word that rhymes with the given word.

1. Tool

Fool
Tear
Tin

2. Fry

Cook
Cry
Fin

3. Duck

Water
Grain
Luck

4. Feet

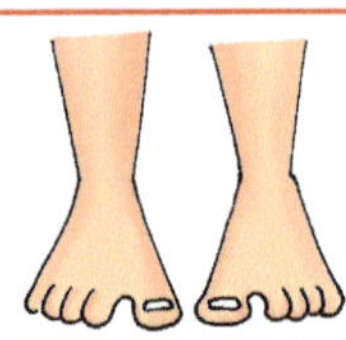

Trees
Breeze
Sheet

5. Cakes

Cooks
Chops
Bakes

6. Play

Can
Man
Day

7. Shine

Fine
Sun
Star

8. Write

Bright
Weight
Book

39. Find Out

Find the following Christmas words in the grid below.

December

Fruitcake

Angels

Mary

Joseph

Gifts

Jesus

Jingle

						A						
						N						
					X	G	M					
					M	E	B					
				Y	A	L	G	V				
			Q	R	R	S	F	W	J			
		S	G	E	Y	S	R	D	E	N		
	J	N	M	I	D	T	U	S	S	J	K	
X	O	O	G	N	E	O	I	L	U	I	O	S
S	S	W	I	D	C	C	T	E	S	N	T	A
T	E	M	F	E	E	K	C	I	N	G	R	N
A	P	A	T	E	M	I	A	G	O	L	E	T
R	H	N	S	R	B	N	K	H	W	E	E	A
					E	G	E					
					R	P	Z					

Tree

Star

Stocking

Snowman

Snow

Sleigh

Reindeer

Santa

40. Replace It

Complete the sentences by replacing the picture clues with the words from the help box.

bed	pizza	cap	Clouds	pen
fox	book	cat	wolf	mouse

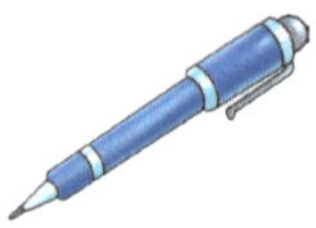

1. I bought a ____________ and a pencil.

2. I found the ____________ under the ____________.

3. We had a ____________ and a sandwich.

4. The ____________ chased the ____________.

5. ________________ covered the sky.

6. The ________________ jumped into the well.

7. The ________________ ate grandmother.

8. Santa wears a ________________ on his head.

41. Connect It

Connect the pictures with the correct word.

Classroom

Bathroom

Plaything

Farm

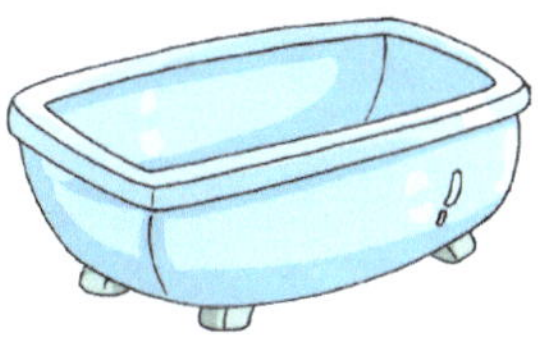

Snow

Animal

Green

Kitchen

42. Circle It

Look at the picture and circle the correct answer.

1. Who read stories to the children every night?
   a. Mother
   b. Father

2. Which pet animal did the children have?
   a. Cat
   b. Dog

3. How did Peter Pan enter the room?
   a. Through the window
   b. Through the door

4. Where did Peter Pan find his shadow?
   a. In a drawer
   b. On a table

5. How did Peter Pan, Wendy and her brothers reach Neverland?
   a. They walked
   b. They flew

6. Who did Peter Pan fight with?
   a. Pirates
   b. Thieves

43. Find Out

What am I?

1. I am the king of beasts
   I like to eat deer meat.
   Who am I?
   ____

2. I have gills.
   I live in water.
   Who am I?
   ____

3. It is shaped like an arc.
   It comes in many colours.
   What is it?
   ____

4. It falls from the sky.
   When it falls, stay indoors
   if you want to stay dry.
   What is it?
   ____

5. I live in a house called a coop.
   I eat worms and bugs,
   and grain.
   Who am I?
   ____

6. I live in the woods.
   I'm very big and furry.
   I like to eat fish and berries.
   Who am I?
   ____

7. I have four legs and webbed feet.
   I can swim in water and hop on land.
   Who am I?
   ____

8. I live in the ocean.
   I have eight legs,
   two big claws and a tail.
   Who am I?
   ____

44. Write It

Write the words given in the help box in the blanks according to their beginning alphabets.

Pin	Say	Yarn	In	Zip
Tell	Eat	Map	Sit	Nip
Out	Real	Bite	Gun	Comb
Win	Dear	Lean	Umbrella	Hit
Fin	Quill	Jump	Van	Kite

M____	L____	D____
J____	W____	G____
P____	V____	R____
E____	B____	Q____
F____	T____	O____
Y____	Z____	S____
K____	H____	S____
U____	C____	N____
	I____	

45. Find Out

Can you find all the words from the picture related to Mowgli and his friends in the grid below?

w	n	t	i	g	e	r	z	k	s	q	j
v	w	c	a	t	t	l	e	b	t	j	g
v	u	h	o	b	a	g	h	e	e	r	a
m	o	w	g	l	i	e	d	t	k	h	e
o	g	i	f	r	s	r	q	b	i	y	i
h	e	j	h	y	g	g	q	t	p	h	s
h	i	l	l	t	o	p	e	s	a	s	q
d	s	j	n	w	j	u	n	g	l	e	p
m	o	o	n	l	i	g	h	t	m	a	r
o	c	u	b	j	v	i	l	l	a	g	e
o	r	a	v	i	n	e	t	a	a	o	t
h	u	a	k	e	l	a	v	s	h	o	k

46. Letter Fun

Identify these pictures and circle the alphabet they start from.

C A D

R G T

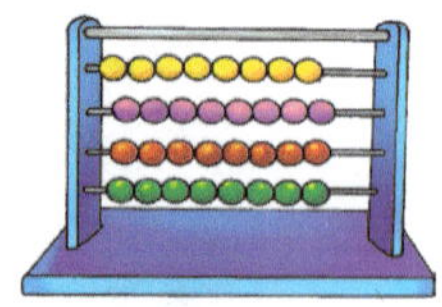

S T A

R H D

F O T

W P L

R T F

D R C

S C T

B A G

F B V

G R B

H Y U

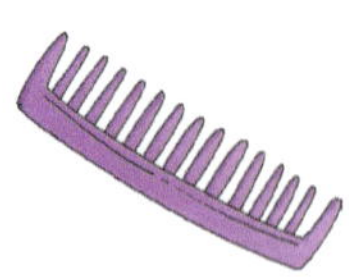

T S C

I M P

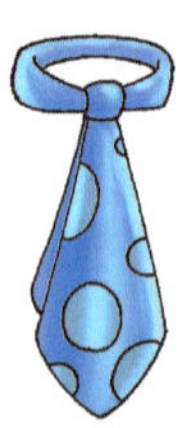

T A P

P L O

Y T P

47. Circle It

Circle the largest image in each row.

48. Missing Letter

Fill in the missing letters to complete the words.

C_N_LE

A_G_L

SN_W_AN

GA_LA_D

C_OK_ES

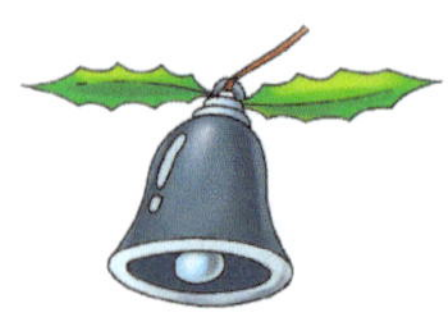

B_L_

CH_R_H

ST_CKI_G

RE_ND_ER

T_E_

S_A_F

SN_WFLA_E

49. Sentence Fun

Look at the pictures and choose the correct word to complete the sentences.

mouse	lion	tortoise
crow	fox	hunter

1. The hare and the __________  decided to have a race.

2. The town __________  went to the countryside to meet the country mouse.

3. When the __________  was fast asleep, a mouse entered the cave.

4. The thirsty __________  was looking for water on a hot summer day.

5. The thirsty __________  fell into the well.

6. One day a ________  came to the forest.

50. Listen and Follow

For each set of pictures, read aloud the instructions and follow the directions.

Draw a circle around the box and a line under the chair.

Draw a line under the bottle and a circle around the glass.

Draw a circle around the scarf and a square around the necktie.

51. Fill Up

The names and objects in the pictures are mismatched. Cross out the incorrect name and write the correct name.

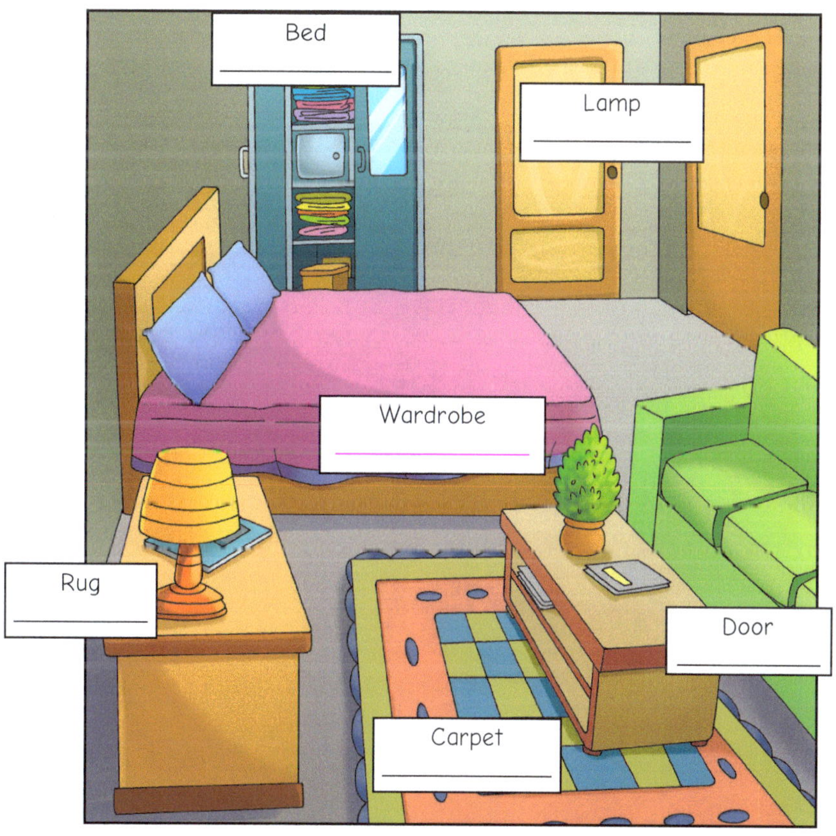

52. Rhyming Fun

Choose the correct letters to complete the rhyming words.

F A P T C	 _AN	 _AN
P S D N T	 _NAIL	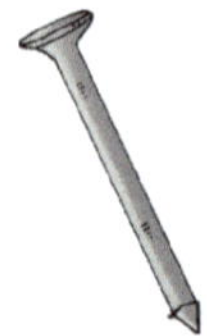 _AIL
B S T P L	 _ALLOON	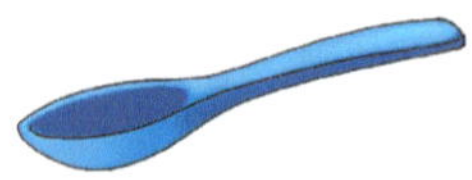 _POON
T Y R S L	 _AKE	 _NAKE
O U R P T	 _RAIN	 _LANE
J K F B C	 _LOCK	 _LOCK

53. ABC

Draw a line following the letters in the alphabetical order to help the hen reach its pen for the night.

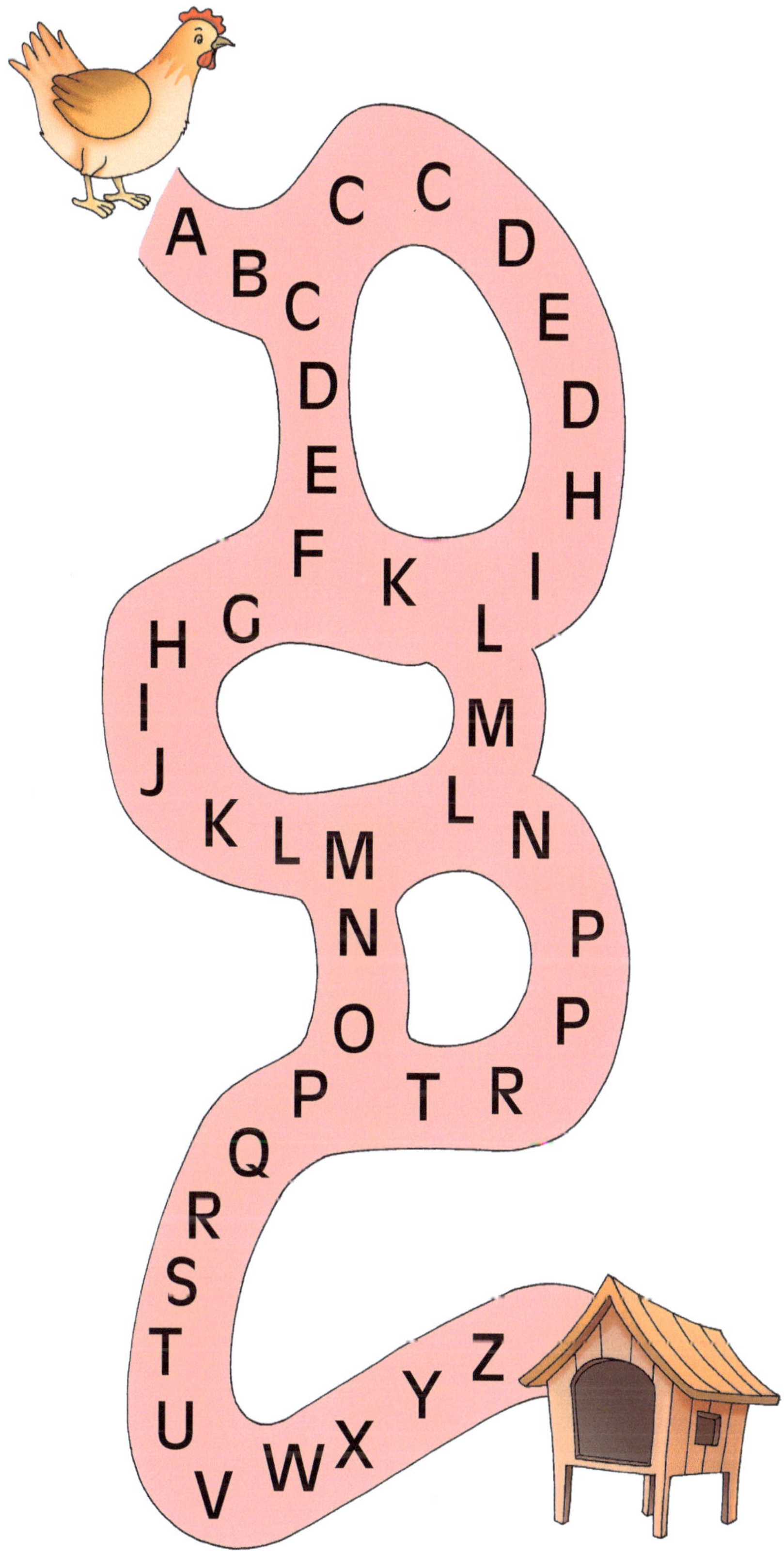

54. Letter Fun

Look at the pictures carefully and say their name. Now circle the letter that the name of the picture begins with.

 C P D	 R G Q	 R T A
 H W D	 F A T	 B P L
 R T B	 A R C	 S F T
 D U B	 F B V	 G R L
 F Y U	 T S C	 I R P
 T A P	 C L O	 Y T B

55. Circle It

Circle the smallest in each row.

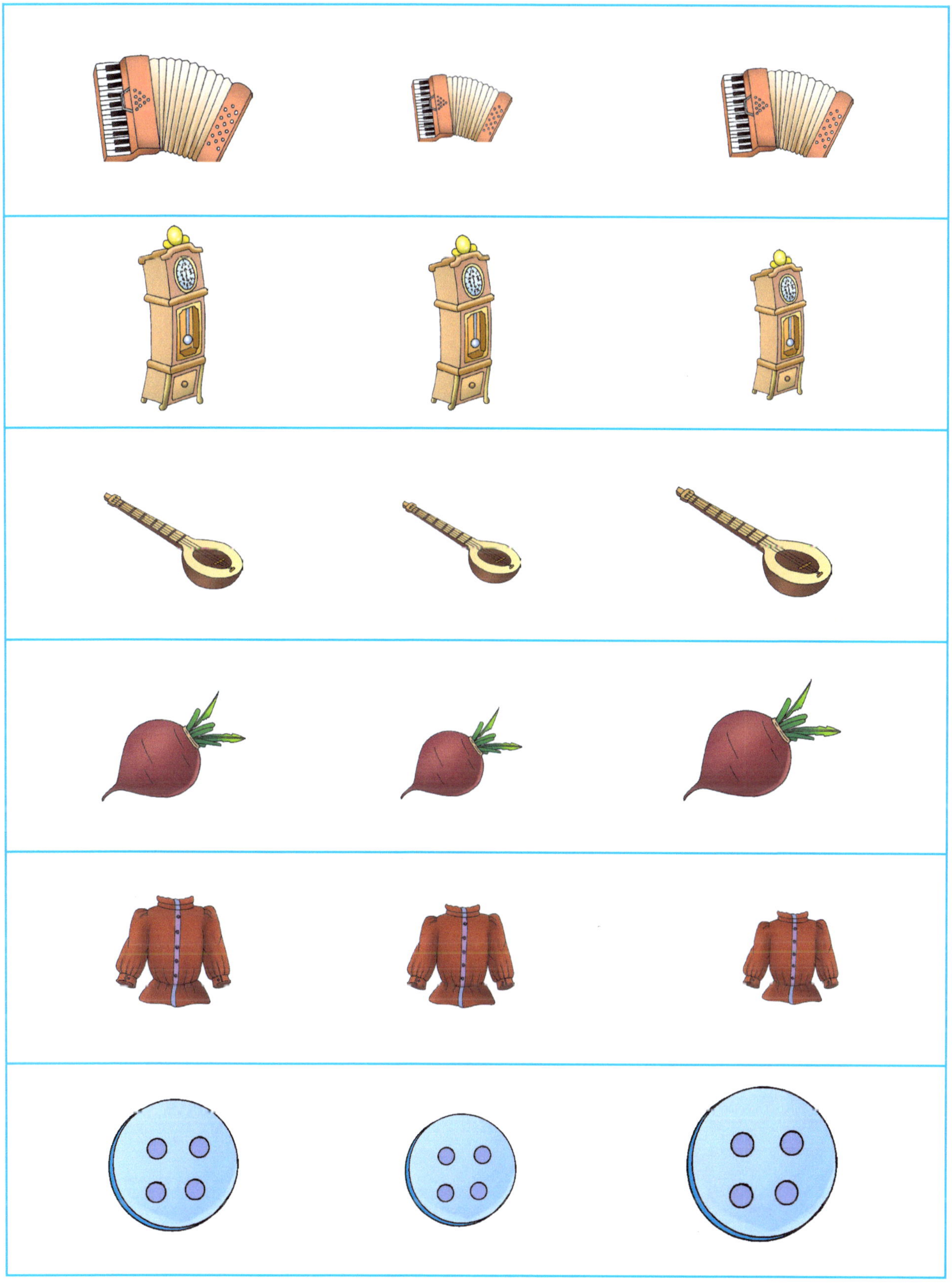

56. Missing Letter

Fill in the missing letters to complete the words.

AC_OBA_

MA_ICIA_

E_EPHA_T

ME_RY-GO-RO_ND

C_O_N

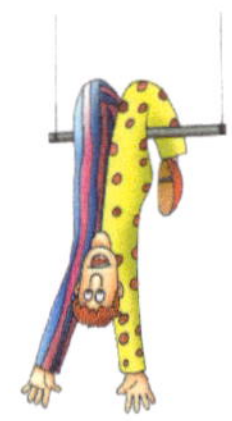

G_MNA_T

JU_GLE

TE_T

TI_KE_

U_ICY_LE

MO_KE_

CO_TON CA_DY

57. Complete It

Look at the picture clues and choose the correct word to complete the sentences.

umbrella	elephant	boy
aeroplane	owl	duck

1. The __________  is swimming in the pond.

2. The __________  is flying in the sky.

3. The __________  is playing football.

4. The man is walking with an _________. 

5. The __________  is pushing the car.

6. The __________  is sitting on the tree.

58. Listen and Follow

For each set of pictures, read aloud the instructions and follow the directions.

Draw a circle around the guitar and a line under the flute.

Draw a ball by the bat and a circle around the football.

Draw a line under the computer and a circle around the mobile phone.

59. Spying Fun

The wind blew away Daisy's clothes. Can you help her?

60. Choose It

Choose the correct letters to complete the rhyming words.

H T V D P	 __EN	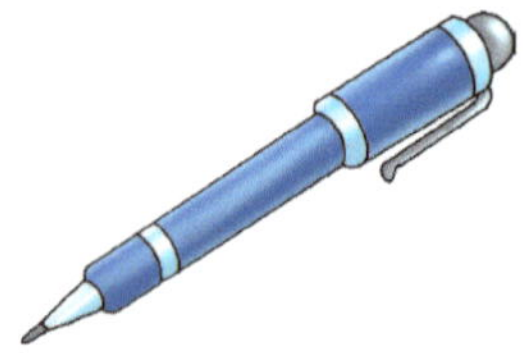 __EN
B R P D C	 __HAIR	 __EAR
L F T Y I	 __ROG	 __OG
M H J V P	 __OUSE	 __OUSE
E D F C B	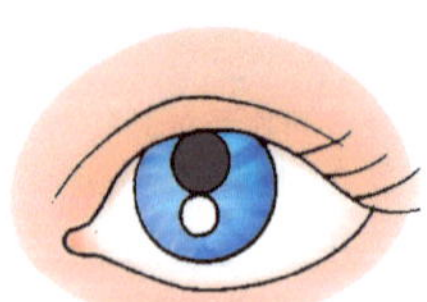 __YE	 __LY
L P D S C	 __LOCK	 __OCK

61. ABC

Fill in the blanks with the missing letter to complete each series.

1.	D	_	F	G	H
2.	J	K	L	_	N
3.	_	S	T	U	V
4.	Q	_	S	T	U
5.	H	I	J	_	L
6.	F	_	H	I	J
7.	G	H	_	J	K
8.	_	P	Q	R	S

62. Letter Fun

Look at the pictures carefully and say their name. Now circle the letter that the name of the picture begins with.

C P S

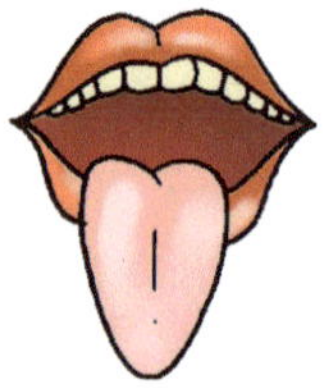

R T Q

R T D

H V D

P A T

B P J

R L B

A R S

S F L

K U G

F B E

G B L

F C U

T S D

I R F

T A P

C R O

S T B

63. Circle It

Circle the thickest in each row.

64. Missing Letter

Fill in the missing letters to complete the words.

S_OV_

BI_THD_Y

F_AG

GRA_DMOT_ER

M_ON

ST_E_T

S_AI_S

P_A_T

B_BY

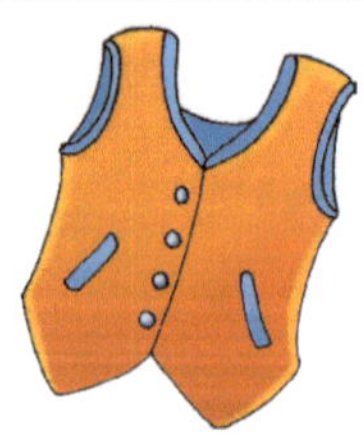

VE_T

T_U_K

R_CK

65. Listen and Follow

For each set of pictures, read aloud the instructions and follow the directions.

Draw a cross on the shirt and a line under the jacket.

Draw a square around the tiger and a circle around the lion.

Draw a circle around the cup and a line under the pan.

66. The Forest

Look at the pictures and choose the correct word to complete the sentences.

fox	rabbit	rhinoceros
elephant	deer	coconut

One day, a ________  was sleeping under a coconut tree.

Suddenly, there was a huge THUD! A big ______  had fallen on the ground.

The rabbit woke up and ran as fast as he could.

The rabbit saw a ________  and said, 'The Earth is cracking up. Run to save your life!'

And so the deer began to run too.

Next they saw a ________  and it joined them too.

Very soon an ________  joined them.

Next it was a ________ , and then a peacock joined too.

Earth	coconut	ground
animals	lion	rabbit

Soon all the animals ran past the lion's den. On hearing their screams, the ______  came out of his den and asked, 'Why are you all running?'

'Oh, King Lion,' the animals cried, 'The ________  is cracking up!'

'Who saw it cracking up?' asked the lion.

The rabbit told him how he had heard a big THUD, and how the _________ 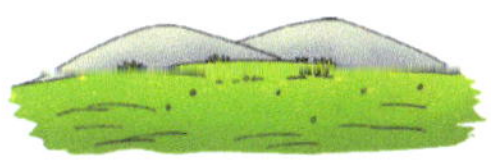 shook!

'Take me to the place. I want to see what the matter is,' the lion said.

When the lion and all the animals reached the spot where the rabbit was sleeping, the lion saw a huge __________  lying on the ground. The clever lion understood what had happened!

The lion said to the ______ , 'Why, you fool! It must have been the sound of the coconut falling to the ground which made the Earth shake.'

All the ________  laughed at their own foolishness and returned home.

67. Spying Fun

Mother monkey has lost her baby monkeys. Can you help her find them?

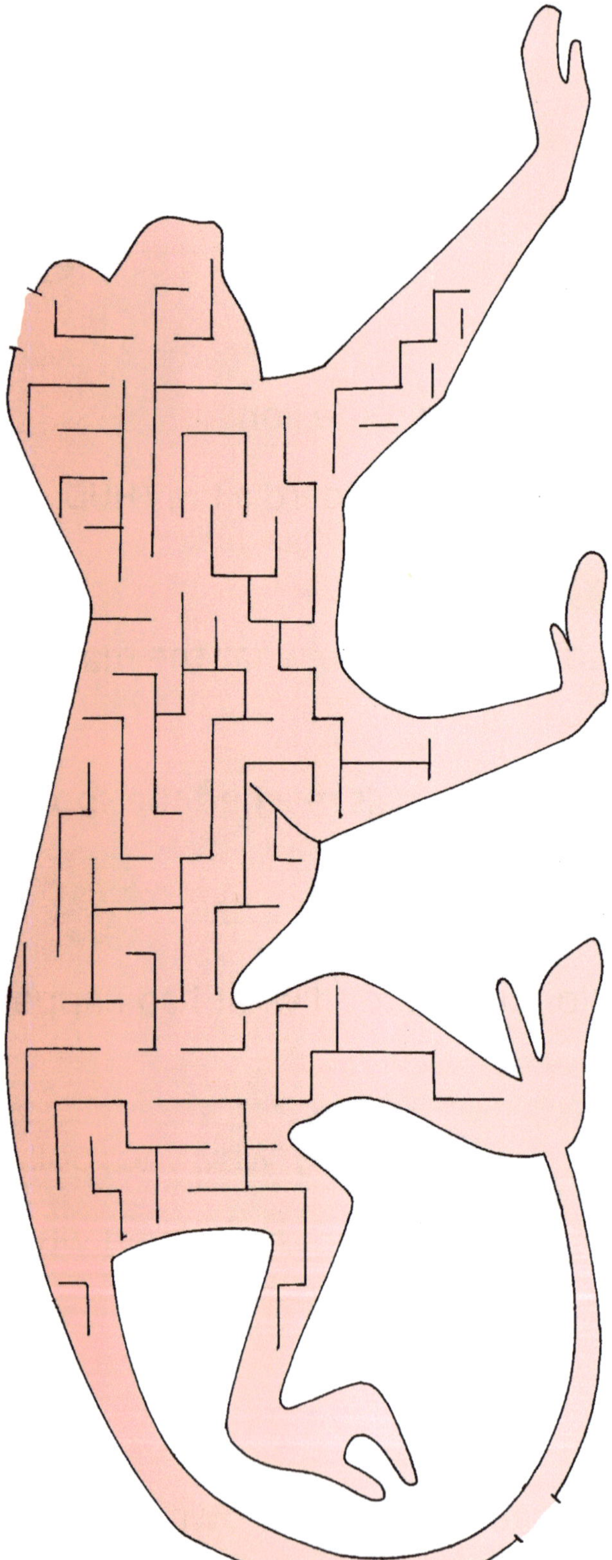

68. Circle It

Circle the picture that rhymes with the picture in the first column.

 BEES	 CHEESE	 CHAIR	 CAR
 RING	 WHALE	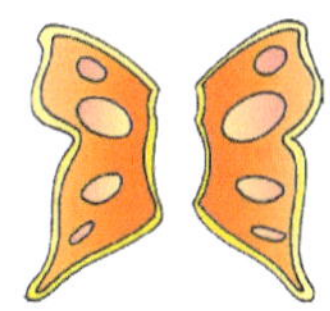 WING	 BIRD
 FOX	 CAT	 DOG	 BOX
 CAT	 HAT	 NET	 WOOL
 BOAT	 PUP	 GOAT	 JUG
 PARROT	 HARE	 ONION	 CARROT

69. Complete the Series

Fill in the blanks with correct letters to complete the series.

mno___	qrs___	uvw___
ddee___	ffgg___	hhii___
aabb___	cc___ee	eeff___
abc___	efg___	ijk___
pqr___	stu___	vwx___
dfh___	lnp___	tvx___
f___hi	j___lm	n___pq
ttuu___	vvww___	xxyy___

70. First Letter

Look at the pictures carefully and say their name. Now circle the letter that the name of the picture begins with.

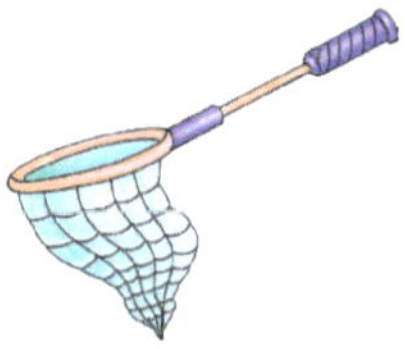
D N P

D C S

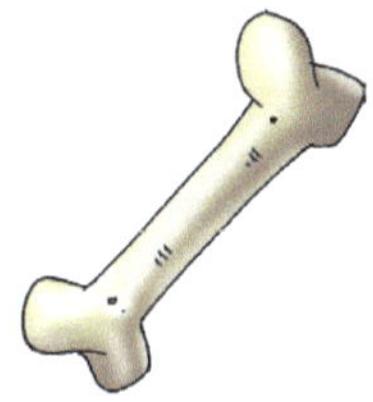
Y B C

O V B

A S N

M C D

F L S

A R C

A K P

M C W

A S Y

P U L

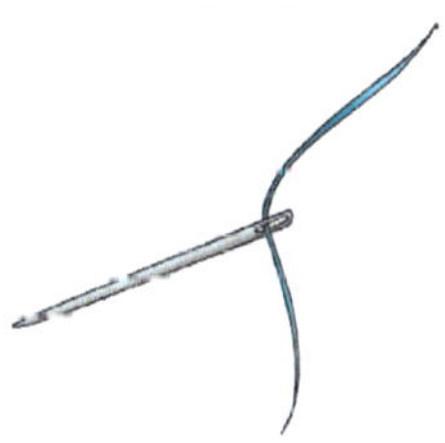
A N P

T M D

I C X

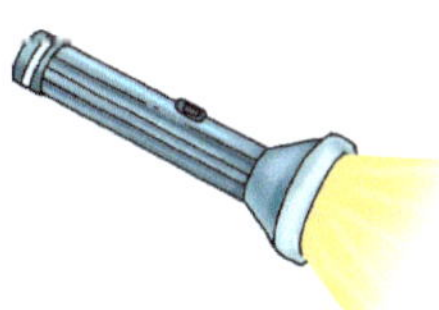
S F T

D U O

F A B

71. Tallest of All

Circle the tallest in each row.

72. Fill In

Fill in the missing letters to complete the words.

TOA_TER

KE_TLE

O_EN

PA_

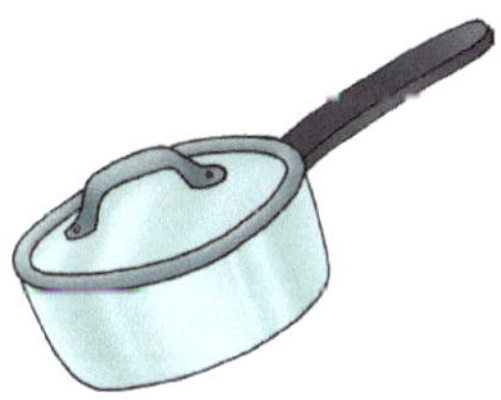

SAUCE_AN

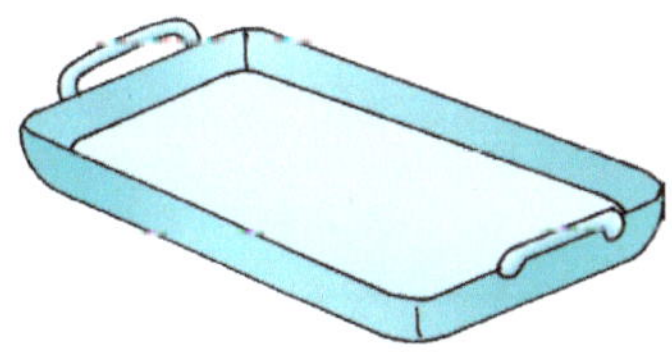

DI_H

SI_K

BO_L

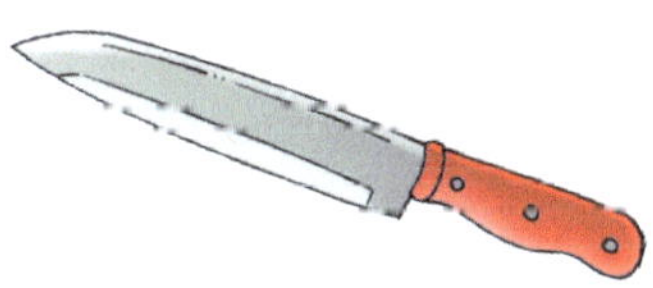

K_IFE

TEA_OT

LA_LE

A_RON

73. Sentence Fun

Look at the pictures and choose the correct word to complete the sentences.

cat	sink	pillow
swing	couch	car

1. The ____________  is in the living room.

2. The ____________  is on the bed.

3. The ____________  is in the kitchen.

4. The ____________  is in the garden.

5. The ____________  is sleeping on the couch.

6. The ____________  is in the garage.

74. Listen and Follow

For each set of pictures, read aloud the instructions and follow the directions.

Draw a basket under the apple and a spoon beside the cake.

Draw some food on the plate and a circle around the table.

Draw some grass by the cow and a line under the monkey.

75. Spying Fun

Find the following things in the picture below.

Candy	Balloon	Cake	Cookies
Gift	Candle	Pizza	Ribbon

76. Circle It

Circle the picture that rhymes with the picture in the first column.

 Cake	 Snake	 Tree	 Bucket
 Bag	 Gun	 Kettle	 Flag
 Jam	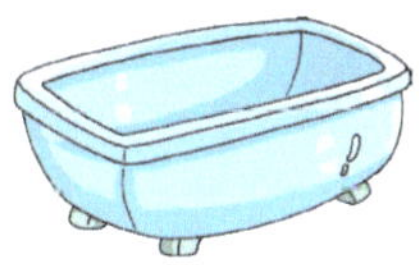 Tub	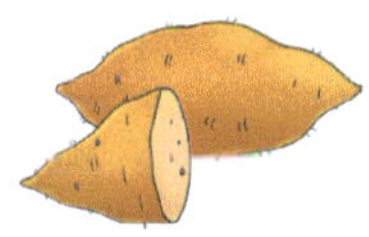 Yam	 Van
 Fat	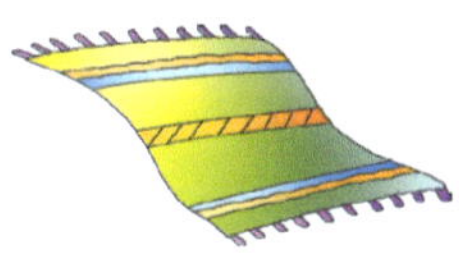 Mat	 Bed	 Red
 Sea	 Gate	 Beach	 Flea
 King	 Swing	 Queen	 Prince

77. Letter Fun

Look at the pictures carefully and say their name. Now circle the letter that the name of the picture begins with.

O A P

G C S

W B D

R V G

A C N

R S D

F L S

S L C

G W A

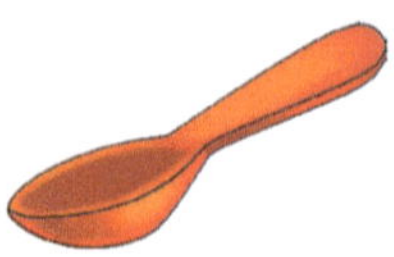

D C S

P R H

P C L

C N P

R B H

R C Q

C F P

C D O

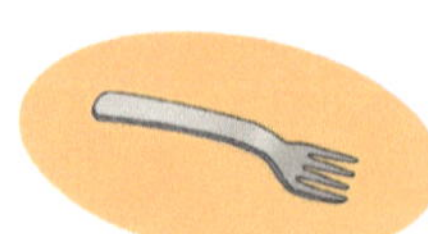

F T J

78. Missing Letter

Fill in the missing letters to complete the words.

ENV_L_PE

_X

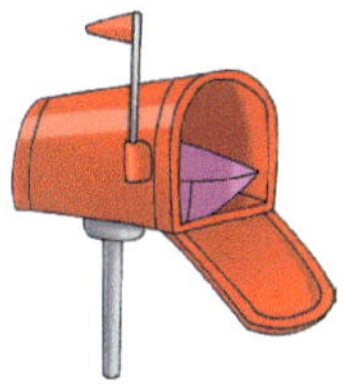

M_ILB_X

T_LEVIS_ON

TR_CT_R

B_RN

W_LL

AMB_LANC_

TR_FF_C L_GHT

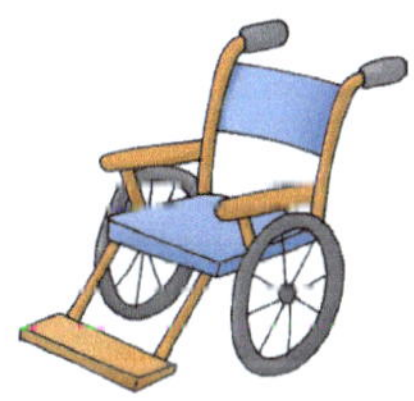

WH_ELCH_IR

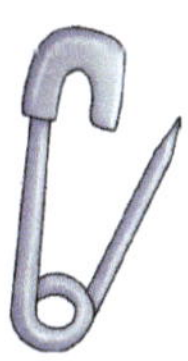

SAF_TY P_N

TEL_PH_NE

79. Draw It

For each set of pictures, read aloud the instructions and follow the directions.

Draw a circle around the object that can fly and a line under the book.

Draw a square around the pen and a line under the table.

Draw a circle around the bag and a line under the motorcycle.

80. Spying Fun

Find the following things in the picture below.

Car	Flashlight	Ice Cream	Dog
Apple	Pen	Camera	Book

81. Rhyming Fun

Circle the picture that rhymes with the picture in the first column.

 STAR	 SHOE	 SOCKS	 CAR
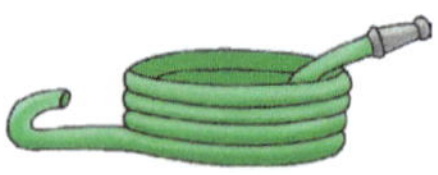 HOSE	 TRAIN	 NOSE	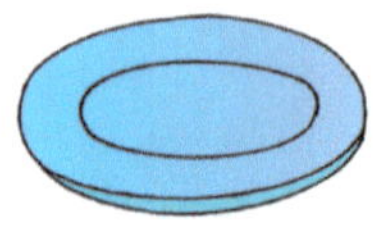 PLATE
 FROG	 DOG	 ANT	 SAND
 TRUCK	 GIFT	 DUCK	 BAG
 BOWL	 MOLE	 FAN	 TREE
 MOON	 BOOK	 DOOR	 SPOON

82. First Letter

Look at the pictures carefully and say their name. Now circle the letter that the name of the picture begins with.

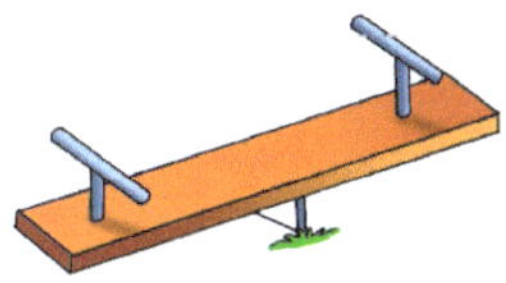 S P R	 R T A	 R T C
 H V B	 P Y T	 B C D
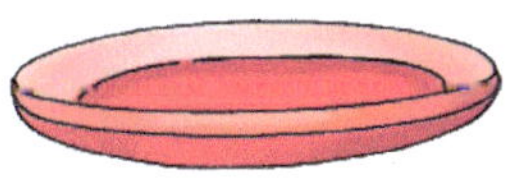 R L D	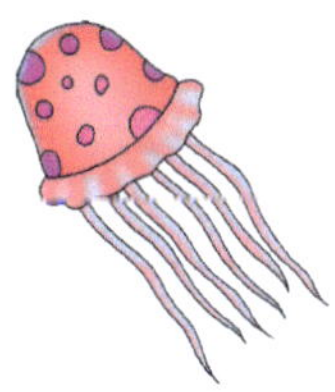 A J S	 T K L
 M U P	 U P E	 G B L
 F B S	 T M D	 I N T
 T A O	 D T O	 R T W

83. Thinnest of All

Circle the thinnest in each row.

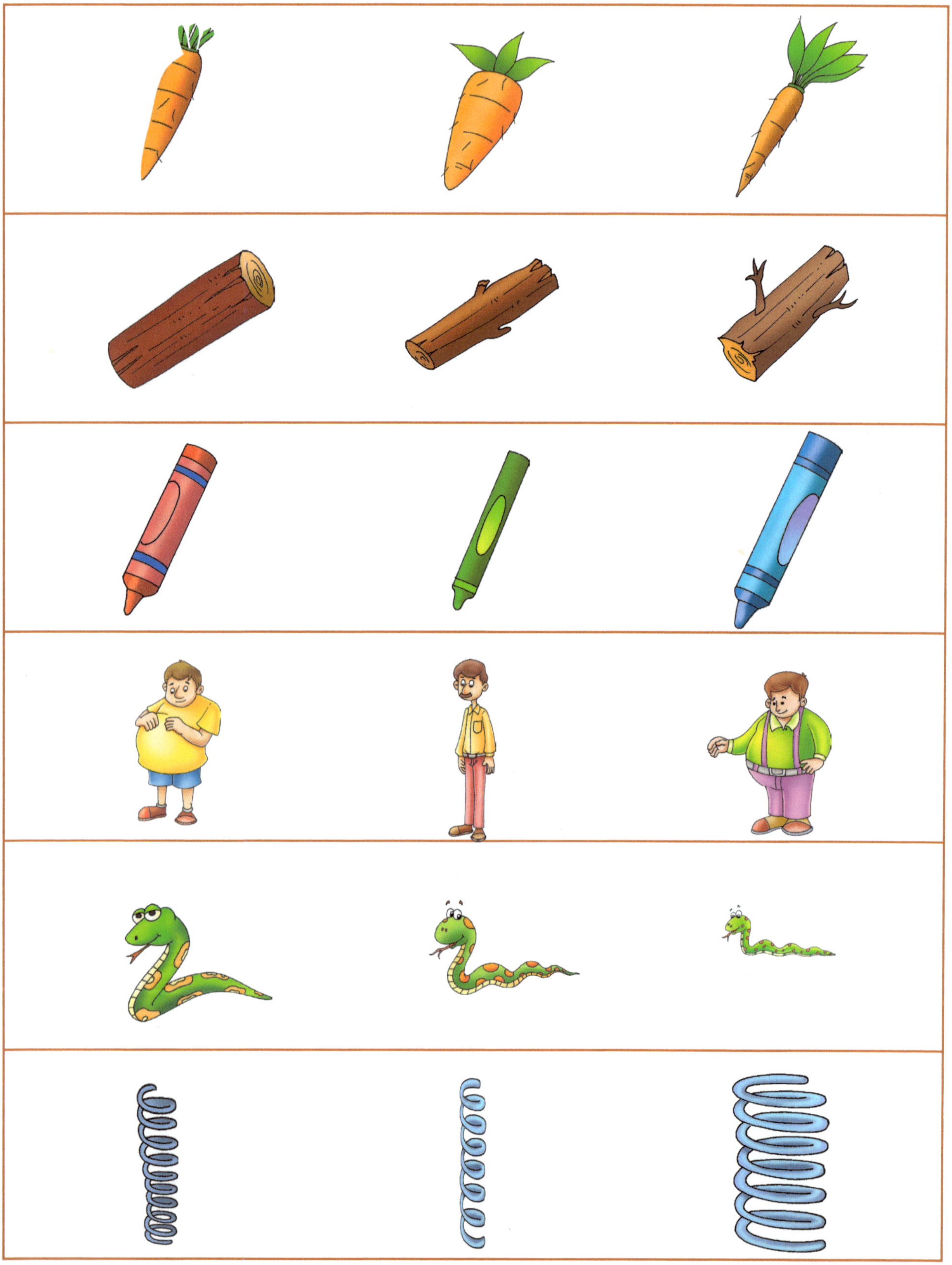

84. Name the Body Parts

Fill in the blanks with the correct name of the body part.

Chest	Mouth	Fingers	Stomach	Nose
Eye	Thigh	Knee	Eyebrow	Arm
Foot	Neck	Toe	Forehead	Ear

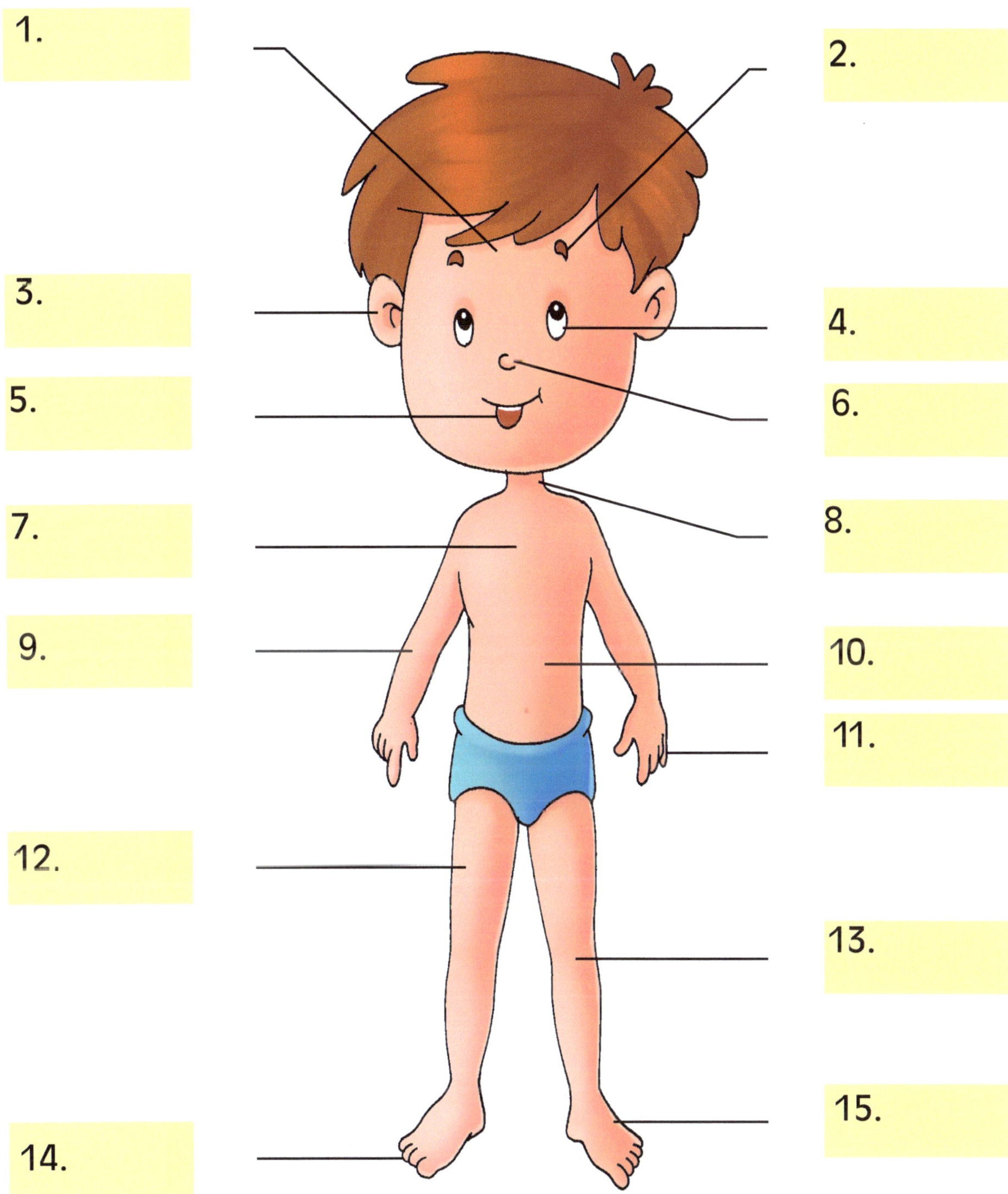

85. Picture Clues

Look at the pictures and choose the correct word to complete the sentences.

star	stockings	reindeer
snow	snowman	doll

1. Father bought a ______  and a Christmas tree.

2. The __________  pulled the sleigh.

3. The boy hung the _____  over the fireplace.

4. The girls made a ________  .

5. The children played in the _______  .

6. Mother put a ______  on the tree.

86. Listen and Follow

For each set of pictures, read aloud the instructions and follow the directions.

Draw a line below the glass and a circle around the cup.

Draw a square beside the bag and a triangle above the car.

Draw a line under the star and a circle around the sun.

87. Spying Fun

Find the following objects in the illustration.

Globe	Map	Scissors	Crayons

88. Missing Letter

Fill in the missing letters to complete the words.

C_NE

B_O_S

S_IRT

H_T

_UD_ING

TE_EP_ONE

WA_CH

_USH

_AMP

E_TI_G

R_NNI_G

T_ACT_R

Answers

1. Do the Chores

Wash	Iron	Water	Sow
Clean	Sweep	Mop	Rake
Mow	Dust		

2. Order It

Shorts - 4	Shirt - 3
Skirt - 5	Pants - 2
Socks - 6	Shoes - 7
Gloves - 1	Tie - 8

3. Circle It

1. behind 2. under 3. in
4. between 5. in front of 6. on

4. Find Out

c	g	a	g	l	o	p	v	k	n	t	q	i	l	n
o	i	f	d	j	u	x	u	l	s	h	f	a	f	k
o	n	u	j	x	p	y	t	r	u	f	f	l	e	t
k	g	g	c	u	p	c	a	k	e	t	p	a	b	j
l	e	e	m	s	k	q	h	p	y	c	a	k	e	e
e	r	p	v	l	f	v	s	w	r	a	t	x	h	l
x	b	a	x	q	r	x	o	e	w	b	d	a	q	l
v	r	s	e	j	b	e	u	z	p	i	e	l	b	y
m	e	t	c	t	w	a	f	f	l	e	g	b	w	h
n	a	r	l	c	s	j	f	w	j	a	m	r	y	p
s	d	y	a	p	f	b	l	c	n	i	g	o	l	v
c	y	o	i	h	c	t	e	t	a	r	t	w	c	n
o	f	c	r	p	u	d	d	i	n	g	h	n	g	a
n	f	u	d	g	e	o	v	v	b	z	k	i	q	z
e	v	g	p	h	m	u	f	f	i	n	i	e	w	y

5. Fill Up

Foxes	Turkeys	Potatoes
Volanoes	Roofs	Wives
Berries	Cities	

6. Add Meaning to It

The cat is in the hat.
The boy is swimming.
The girl is running.
The man is cooking.
The doll is sitting on the chair.
The bird is flying.

7. Describe It

Full moon	Big castle
Wicked witch	Good fairy
Sweet candy	Black cat
White ghost	Wild lion
Dark night	Long stockings
Haunted house	Scary spider
Round pumpkin	Hot soup

8. Complete It

1. Hair	2. Mouth
3. Fingers	4. Eye
5. Nose	6. Tongue
7. Hand	8. Toe
9. Stomach	10. Leg
11. Head	12. Arm

9. Fill Up

1. slowly	2. quickly
3. loudly	4. bravely
5. happily	6. carefully

10. Connect It

Tall ⟷ Short
Loud ⟷ Quiet
Slow ⟷ Fast
Dark ⟷ Light
None ⟷ All
Old ⟷ New

11. Circle It

A cow	A milkmaid
A hen	An egg
An elephant	A leaf
A camel	A desert
An ape	A rainforest
A yak	A mountain

12. Find Out

Roar	Meow	Bark	Croak
Quack	Hiss	Hoot	Bleat

13. Write It

Hoe Seeds Pots Rake
Watering can Shovel

14. Name It

Rose	Sunflower	Dahlia	Daisy
Tulip	Marigold	Daffodil	

15. Spell It

Eight	Height	Broccoli	Forty
Friend	Ninth	Balloon	Happily

16. Guess It

1. Fire engine	2. Raindrop
3. Crosswalk	4. Basketball
5. Seashell	6. Pancake
7. Cheesecake	8. Meatball

17. Fill Up

Sweets (c)	Milk (u)
Apple (c)	Grapes (c)
Cheese (u)	Bread (c)
Water (u)	Teacup (c)
Chair (c)	Pizza (c)
Flour (u)	Bee (c)

18. Connect It

Telephone → Thing
Mount Everest → Name
Gorilla → Animal
Computer → Thing
River → Place
Tailor → Name
Porcupine → Animal
Soldier → Name

19. Circle It

Foal	Calf	Piglet	Gosling
Joey	Pup	Tadpole	Fry

20. Crossword

Across	Down
1. Cabbage	1. Cauliflower
4. Broccoli	2. Garlic
7. Mushroom	3. Potato
8. Peas	5. Pumpkin
9. Onion	6. Tomatoes
10. Carrot	

21. Complete It

SLEEP	JUGGLE	PUSH
CRY	WALK	DANCE
JUMP	LISTEN	FLY
READ	LAUGH	KICK

22. Group It

Words with A

Apron Aeroplane
Axe Angel

Words with B

Boat Bib
Brush Banana

Words with C

Cherry Cactus
Clock Cloud

Words with D

Door Dolphin
Duck Doll

23. Find Out

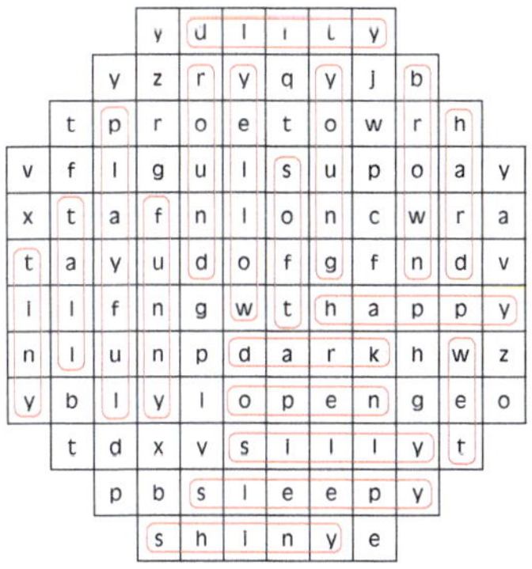

24. Fill Up

IJUV LMN RST
CDE OPQ GHI

STU JKL KLM
FGH NOP QRS

IJK BCD
MNO HIJ

25. Circle It

Flowers Bowl Coat
Blocks Brushes Horse
Butterfly Queen Zebras
Fly Fruits Snails
Bat Rings

26. Crossword

Across
2. Peacock
3. Crow
5. Pigeon
7. Penguin
8. Kiwi
9. Ostrich

Down
1. Woodpecker
2. Parrot
4. Duck
6. Goose
9. Owl
10. Toucan

27. Complete It

1. It 2. He 3. She
4. She 5. We 6. They

28. Order It

1. 2, 1, 3 2. 2, 1, 3
3. 2, 1, 3 4. 3, 1, 2

30.

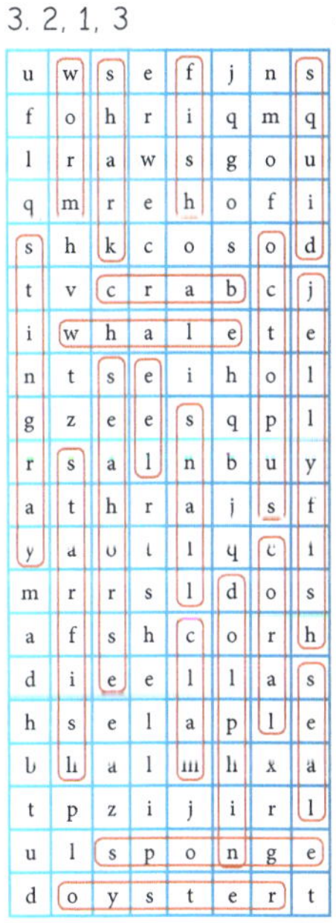

31. Choose It

1. run 2. climb 3. jump
4. swim 5. drive 6. sing
7. crawl 8. sting

32. Name It

HOUSE CLOCK DOCTOR
VIOLIN TIGER LIBRARY
PAINTER CRAYON DONKEY
JUICE SWEATER
BEDROOM

33. 1. A mermaid 2. New clothes
3. It sang 4. Cooked food
5. A pea

34. Circle It

won bye pear flower
hare bear witch sew
stare bee mane knight
sea weigh

35. Crossword

Across
4. Zebra
6. Giraffe
8. Kangaroo
10. Cat
11. Pig

Down
1. Cheetah
2. Frog
3. Dog
5. Elephant
7. Lion
9. Rhino

36. Fill Up

1. What are you doing?
   I am studying.
2. What are you doing?
   I am dancing.
3. What are you doing?
   I am writing.

37. Order It

1. I am a boy.
2. I am a girl.
3. This is a cat.
4. The cat is under the chair.
5. The fox is in the well.
6. The dog is barking.
7. The birds are flying.
8. The starts are shining.

38. Rhyme It

1. Fool 2. Cry 3. Luck 4. Sheet
5. Bakes 6. Clay 7. Fine 8. Bright

39. Find Out

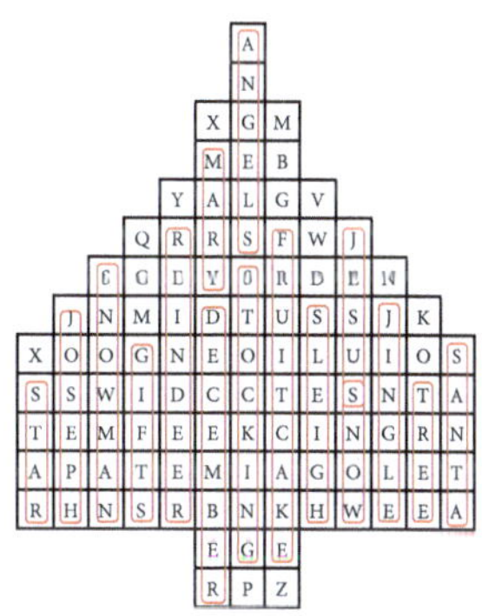

40. Replace It

1. pen 2. book, bed
3. pizza 4. cat, mouse
5. clouds 6. fox
7. wolf 8. cap

42. Circle It

1. a 2. b 3. a 4. a 5. b 6. a

43. Find Out

1. Lion 2. Fish 3. Umbrella
4. Rain 5. Hen 6. Bear
7. Frog 8. Lobster

Answers

44. Write It

map jump pin eat fin yarn kite umbrella	lean win van bite tell zip hit comb in	dear gun real quill out say sit nip

46. Letter Fun

C	R	A
H	F	P
F	D	C
B	B	G
H	C	M
T	O	P

48. Missing Letter

CANDLE	ANGEL
SNOWMAN	GARLAND
COOKIES	BELL
CHURCH	STOCKING
REINDEER	TREE
SCARF	SNOWFLAKE

49. Sentence Fun

1. tortoise
2. mouse
3. lion
4. crow
5. fox
6. hunter

52. Rhyming Fun

FAN	PAN
SNAIL	NAIL
BALLOON	SPOON
RAKE	SNAKE
TRAIN	PLANE
BLOCK	CLOCK

54. Letter Fun

P	Q	R
W	A	B
B	A	F
B	F	L
F	C	R
P	C	B

56. Missing Letter

ACROBAT
MAGICIAN
ELEPHANT
MERRY-GO-ROUND
CLOWN
GYMNAST
JUGGLER
TENT
TICKET
UNICYCLE
MONKEY
COTTON CANDY

58. Complete It

1. duck	2. aeroplane
3. boy	4. umbrella
5. elephant	6. owl

60. Choose It

Hen	Pen
Chair	Bear
Frog	Log
House	Mouse
Eye	Fly
Clock	Lock

61. ABC

1. E	2. M	3. R
4. R	5. K	6. G
7. I	8. O	

62. Letter Fun

S	R	D
V	P	J
L	S	L
G	E	B
C	D	F
P	R	S

64. Missing Letter

STOVE	BIRTHDAY
FLAG	GRANDMOTHER
MOON	STREET
STAIRS	PLANT
BABY	VEST
TRUCK	ROCK

66. The Forest

rabbit, coconut, deer, fox
elephant, rhinoceros, lion
earth, ground, coconut, rabbit
animals

68. Circle It

CHEESE	WING	BOX
HAT	GOAT	CARROT

69. Complete the Series

mnop	qrst	uvwx
ddeeff	ffgghh	hhiijj
aabbcc	ccddee	eeffgg

abcd efgh ijkl
pqrs stuv vwxy
dfhj lnpq tvxz
fghi jklm nopq
ttuuvv vwwxx xxyyzz

70. First Letter

N	C	B
O	S	M
F	C	P
C	S	P
N	M	C
T	D	F

72. Fill In

TOASTER	KETTLE
OVEN	PAN
SAUCEPAN	DISH
SINK	BOWL
KNIFE	TEAPOT
LADLE	APRON

73. Sentence Fun

1. couch	2. pillow
3. sink	4. swing
5. cat	6. car

76. Circle It

snake, flag, yam, mat, flea, swing

77. Letter Fun

P	G	D
G	C	D
S	L	G
S	R	C
C	B	C
F	C	F

78. Missing Letter

ENVELOPE	OX
MAILBOX	TELEVISION
TRACTOR	BARN
WELL	AMBULANCE
TRAFFIC LIGHT	WHEELCHAIR
SAFETY PIN	TELEPHONE

81. Rhyming Fun

car, nose, dog, duck, mole
spoon

82. First Letter

S	A	C
B	P	C
D	J	K
M	P	B
B	M	N
T	T	W

84. Name the Body Parts

1. Forehead	2. Eyebrow
3. Ear	4. Eye
5. Mouth	6. Nose
7. Chest	8. Neck
9. Arm	10. Stomach
11. Fingers	12. Thigh
13. Knee	14. Toe
15. Foot	

85. Picture Clues

1. doll	2. reindeer
3. stockings	4. snowman
5. snow	6. star

88. Missing Letter

CONE	BOOTS
SHIRT	HAT
PUDDING	TELEPHONE
WATCH	PUSH
LAMP	EATING
RUNNING	TRACTOR